olha quanto arróz caiu

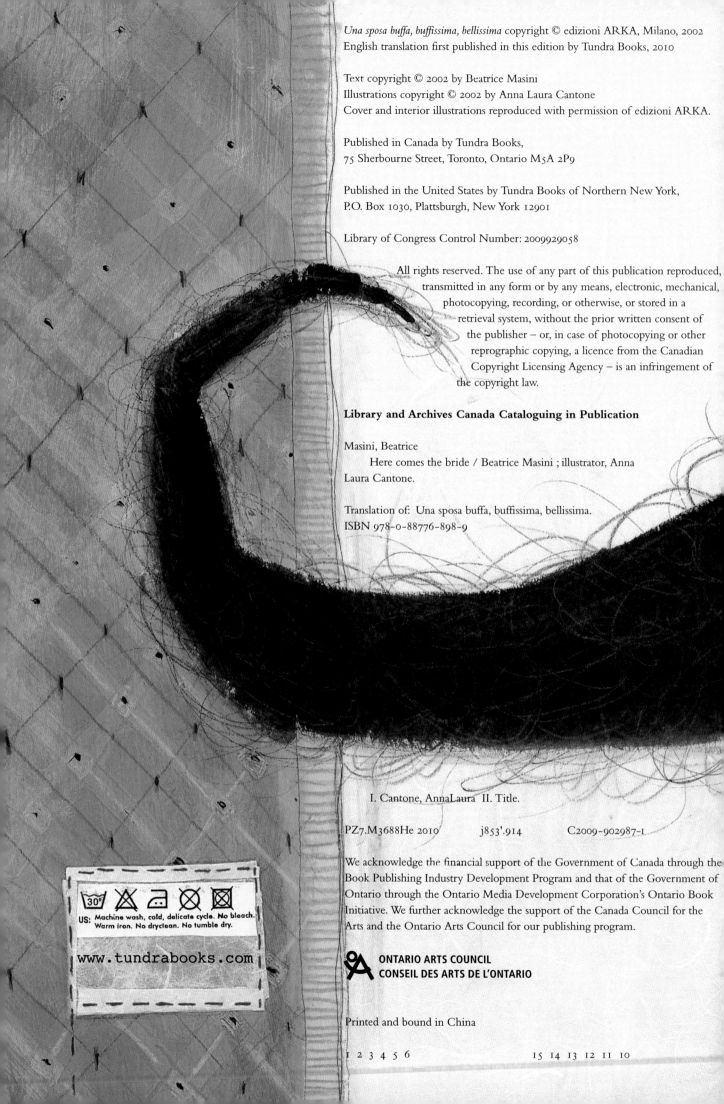

Una sposa buffa, buffissima, bellissima copyright © edizioni ARKA, Milano, 2002
English translation first published in this edition by Tundra Books, 2010

Published in Canada by Tundra Books,
75 Sherbourne Street, Toronto, Ontario M5A 2P9

Published in the United States by Tundra Books of Northern New York,
P.O. Box 1030, Plattsburgh, New York 12901

Library of Congress Control Number: 2009929058

Library and Archives Canada Cataloguing in Publication

Masini, Beatrice
     Here comes the bride / Beatrice Masini ; illustrator, Anna Laura Cantone.

Translation of: Una sposa buffa, buffissima, bellissima.
ISBN 978-0-88776-898-9

I. Cantone, AnnaLaura II. Title.

PZ7.M3688He 2010   j853'.914   C2009-902987-1

We acknowledge the financial support of the Government of Canada through the Book Publishing Industry Development Program and that of the Government of Ontario through the Ontario Media Development Corporation's Ontario Book Initiative. We further acknowledge the support of the Canada Council for the Arts and the Ontario Arts Council for our publishing program.

ONTARIO ARTS COUNCIL
CONSEIL DES ARTS DE L'ONTARIO

US: Machine wash, cold, delicate cycle. No bleach.
Warm iron. No dryclean. No tumble dry.

www.tundrabooks.com

Printed and bound in China

1 2 3 4 5 6   15 14 13 12 11 10

HERE COMES THE BRIDE

Beatrice Masini
Illustrated by Anna Laura Cantone

marie
CATALOGUE
IDEAS
MODA

Wedding

TUNDRA BOOKS

Filomena was a very fine seamstress. With her scissors clashing and needles and thread flashing, she could sew elegant suits and sporty T-shirts and even practical underwear. But her specialty was wedding dresses.

Every bride in town came to Filomena to ask her to make a wedding dress. Filomena would sit in her plain sweater and neat skirt and listen to their dreams.

"Filomena, I want to look like a beautiful princess in flowing satin!"

"Filomena, I want to look like a dainty fairy in delicate lace!"

"Filomena, I want to look like a glamorous movie star in a shimmering silk sheath!"

Filomena listened to each of them and set about turning their dreams into dresses.

ALCINHAS
PANTS
WEDDING
DRESS
A C K E T
Eliza Tinsley
FARFAL
-SHIRT
FASHION DESIGNER
CLOTHING

WEDDING
vestido de noiva
DRESS

total-look

All the while her skillful fingers flew, Filomena
dreamed her own dreams. She longed for the
day when she was the bride.

Anita, her sister, liked to visit Filomena's
studio to gather scraps of pretty fabric to dress
her doll. One day, she heard Filomena sighing.

"If I were sewing my own dress," she said,
"I'd make rosettes to go around my waist. And
bows. Lots of bows. And swags and swags of
silk." Filomena closed her eyes and smiled.

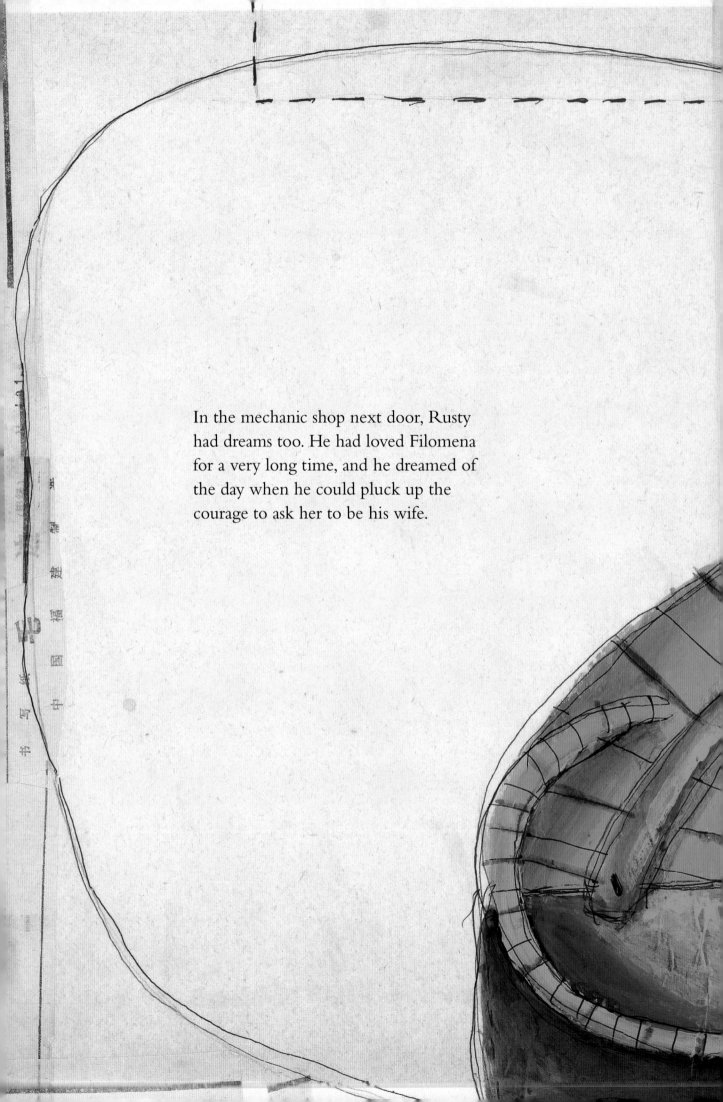

In the mechanic shop next door, Rusty had dreams too. He had loved Filomena for a very long time, and he dreamed of the day when he could pluck up the courage to ask her to be his wife.

When that day finally came, Rusty stood under Filomena's balcony. All in a rush, he called out: "Filomena, you are my one true love! Will you marry me?"

"Tell him yes!" whispered Anita.

Filomena laughed and said in her no-nonsense way, "What took you so long? Of course I will marry you."

getting married
RECÉM
GETTING MARRIED
HEART
CORAÇÃO
COLLANT
FLOR
PHOTO
COLAR
maman
fotografia
HAND-BAG
BOLSA

SAPATOS de NOIVA

37

VESTIDO DE NOIVA

WEDDING
DRESS

And so it was that Filomena could start working on
her own wedding dress. She could put all her dreams
into silk and satin and roses and lace. She had stored
so many ideas while she sewed for other brides!
Maybe too many.

SEAMSTRESS
costureira

Every Sunday, Rusty arrived at Filomena's with
two helmets tucked under his arms. "Let's go
for a ride in the hills on my scooter."

"There'll be time enough for that once
we're married," she would reply. "Today I have
to work on my dress."

So Rusty would mope and take a solitary ride in the hills. "That dress is taking her so long, we'll have grandchildren by the time she finishes it," he would grumble. But he loved his plain, no-nonsense Filomena, and he was prepared to wait.

The big day finally came. The little church was crowded.
Everyone was curious to see the bride's wedding dress.
Filomena had made so many lovely gowns that hers was
bound to be beautiful.

Rusty, dressed in his finest, was nervous and excited as
he waited for Filomena at the church door. He could
imagine her, all wrapped up in her white cloud of a dress.

SPARKLING
PURE **R** ICE
CUBES
IS ONE BAG ENOUGH?

It was more than a cloud. It was a blizzard of white. Her veil was more than a veil. It was a sail. Her flowers were an overgrown garden of hearts and butterflies.

"Where's my sister?" said Anita. "I can't see her."

Filomena was buried in a mountain of silk and satin and lace, rosettes and bows. Her feet, in shiny shoes, peeped out from underneath the swathes of fabric, but nothing else could be seen of Filomena and all Filomena could see was the inside of her veil.

One of the guests chuckled. "She looks like a meringue."
The chuckle turned to laughter. Another guest laughed,
then another, and another, until the whole church was
rocking. Everyone was laughing. Everyone except Rusty.

When he saw that walking mountain of material, he
got frightened. "She'll never fit on my scooter!"

And he did what some people do when they are afraid:
He fled.

Everyone stopped laughing. It's no laughing matter when
a groom flees from the altar.

How strange, thought Filomena. *Why the laughter? And
why the quiet?* She parted the folds and pleats and swags of
her veil. She saw that where Rusty should have been,
Rusty was not. She could hear the sound of a scooter
growing fainter as it raced away from the church.

Filomena hitched up her many skirts and crinolines and ran after Rusty. As she ran, the silk flowers dropped off her dress one by one, but she didn't stop to pick them up. Her veil got caught in the branches of a tree and without a second thought, Filomena tore it off. Her crinolines bunched around her legs so she stepped out of them. She kicked off her dainty shoes (like all brides' shoes, they were too tight for running). All that was left of her poufy dress was a simple shift.

Huffing and puffing, she finally caught up to him.

"I'm sorry! All I was thinking about was my dress, and not you."

"I'm sorry, too. I was scared and forgot that under all that material, there you were."

"Let's go back. Everyone's waiting for us," said Filomena.

"Alright, but we'll have to walk, because you don't have a helmet." It wasn't a very romantic thing to say, but one doesn't always say important things at important moments. The important thing was that Rusty and Filomena returned to town together, hand in hand.

At the reception, nobody could stop talking about Filomena's dress.
It was short, simple, and elegant.
"That's the loveliest dress she's ever made!"